*In the Clouds*

*The Impressions of a Chair*

SARAH BERNHARDT

ILLUSTRATED BY GEORGES CLAIRIN

TRANSLATED BY JOHN JOLINE ROSS

RENARD PRESS

RENARD PRESS LTD

Kemp House
152–160 City Road
London EC1V 2NX
United Kingdom
info@renardpress.com
020 8050 2928

www.renardpress.com

*In the Clouds* first published in French as *Dans les nuages* in 1878
The basis of this translation first published in 1880

Translation, text and notes © Renard Press Ltd, 2021
Extra Material © Renard Press Ltd, 2021

Cover design by Will Dady

Printed in the United Kingdom by Severn

ISBN: 978-1-913724-44-3

9 8 7 6 5 4 3 2 1

The pictures in this volume are reprinted with permission or are presumed to be in the public domain. Every effort has been made to ascertain their copyright status, and to acknowledge this status where required, but we will be happy to correct any errors, should any unwitting oversights have been made, in subsequent editions.

All rights reserved. This publication may not be
reproduced, stored in a retrieval system or transmitted, in any form
or by any means – electronic, mechanical, photocopying, recording
or otherwise – without the prior permission of the publisher.

## CONTENTS

| | |
|---|---|
| *In the Clouds* | 7 |
| Note on the Text and Illustrations | 79 |
| Notes | 79 |
| Biographical Note | 85 |

**IMPRESSIONS D'UNE CHAISE**

Récit recueilli par

*Sarah-Bernhardt*

TO MONSIEUR HENRY GIFFARD

*from two grateful artists*

SARAH BERNHARDT
GEORGES CLAIRIN

My straws were born in a modest field near Toulouse, and my back and legs were taken from a little ash tree in the forest of Saint Germain.

My thoughtful, dreamy nature was forever transporting me into the highest regions.

I longed for luxury, for travel; I envied those gilt chairs whose feet rest on oriental rugs. Being an official chair would have been the delight of my life. The furniture-movers' vans* made my heart beat fast when I saw them driving through the street, loaded down with furniture and chairs which were being carried away to be transported across the seas.

Happy chairs!

And I cried in silence while I hung upside down from an iron bar near the ceiling of a little shop, my tears trickling down, drop by drop, making the gas jet below me crackle.

'What nasty wood!' said the grumbling old dame, the owner of the little shop.

It was a Tuesday. A stout gentleman walked into the shop.

'I would like some chairs,' he said. 'Some cheap chairs.'

It appears that we were cheap, for the shopkeeper displayed twenty-four of my companions.

'That's your affair,' she said. 'How about these?'

'Very well,' said the man, 'but I need more.'

The grumbling old dame showed him thirty more.

'Here is all my stock. Ah! There's this chair too – but I warn you, for I never deceive my customers, it is made of bad wood. The wood is green – it cries all the time!'

'Give it to me anyway,' said the man.

So, here I am, taken away in a big wagon. I traverse many streets, and after that a grand boulevard; the wagon enters an immense courtyard and stops in front of a gate.

We were unloaded from the wagon, and two days later we were placed three by three around marble-topped tables, on which were placed women's portraits and advertisements for pharmacists.

I watch; I listen. I am, it appears, in the courtyard of the Tuileries,* which has become the home of the captive balloon.

'What luck! A balloon!' I saw a balloon, and it was the very largest that had ever been constructed. And then there was a great machine that kept going, going, going all the while. It seems all this was quite superb, for I heard very competent men around me saying, 'It's admirable! Giffard is a truly remarkable man – what a genius organisation!'

I was proud. I didn't know Monsieur Giffard, but that didn't matter – I was proud, all the same. There were people here and there who criticised the cable, the basket, the steam engine, but I quickly came to understand that these detractors were cowards, who made themselves critics because they couldn't be actors.

I laughed behind my straws at all these little weaknesses! One of them said he wouldn't go up because he wished to preserve a husband for his wife; another a father for his children; a third because he was dizzy! And so on – a thousand dull pretexts.

However, I was there for eight days, and the crowd increased with every ascent. Ah! How I would have liked to go up in the balloon too! But no, the passengers always stood up in the basket, so there was no hope for a poor chair.

I was deep in thought one day, but was drawn out of my reverie by the conversation of some men nearby.

'Who are you waving to?'

'Doña Sol.'*

'Ah! Point her out to me – I don't know her.'

'She's coming over.'

I looked over, and I saw, advancing slowly, surrounded by lots of people, a young woman, rather pale and thin. She held a little cane, and was speaking terribly fast. She went up in the balloon, and then, after the ascent, came and sat down very close to me. She was in raptures – she would come again the following day, and every day, every day! This pleased me greatly – I would very much like to serve as her seat.

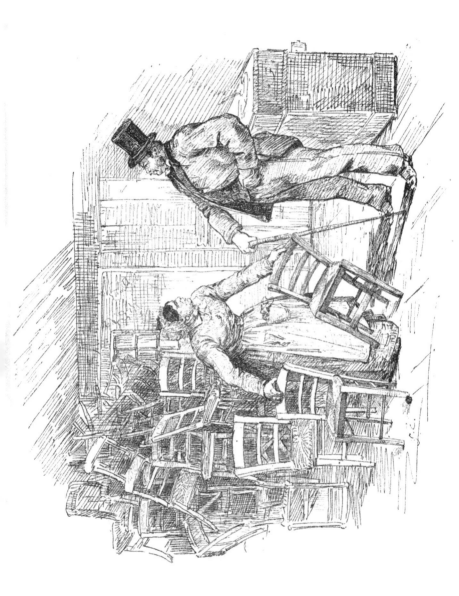

In fact, she did return, and went up in the balloon two or three times each day. I found that a little much. Everybody else seemed to agree with me, and they told her so.

'My chest hurts a little,' she replied, 'and I breathe so much better up there!'

Her voice was so charming that I instinctively agreed with her; but it's a wicked and sneering world, and I heard my young friend criticised, defamed, slandered. I was enraged because I was powerless to come to her defence.

One day a stout gentleman, accompanied by an even larger lady, was unsparing in his abuse – she was a poser, desperate to be the centre of attention, she had no talent as an actress – there was someone unknown who voiced her roles, and she merely mimed! It was a poor sculptor, dying of hunger, who made all her statues in hiding – and as for her paintings, everyone knew they couldn't be her work, for she had never even held a brush! That was *clear, huh*? And they both shook with laughter at this brutal pun.* I jumped in anger, and upset the stout gentleman, who, furious, got up off me, took me by the shoulders and threw me to the ground violently.

'What a horrible chair! It would scarcely support Doña Sol!'*

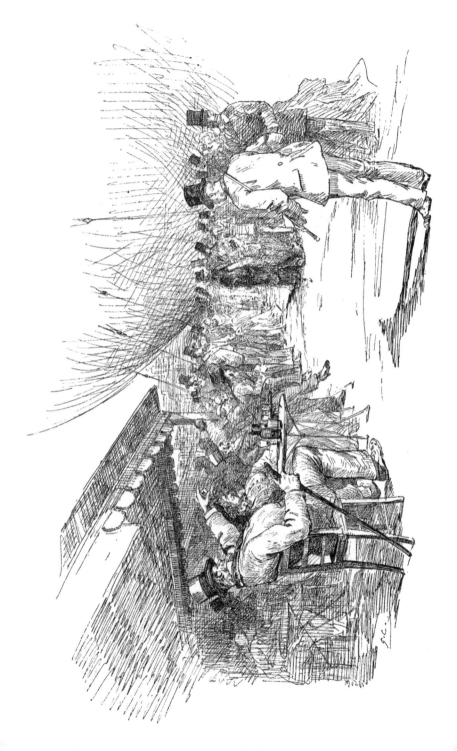

'Wait – that's an idea!' exclaimed Louis Godard,* who was passing by at that moment. 'It's light – we can take it with us tomorrow.' And, picking me up, he examined my limbs to make sure that the brute hadn't broken any part of me. Then he carried me into a large hangar.

'Leave this chair here,' he said, placing me in a corner. 'Doña Sol will use it tomorrow.'

I remained in a reverie. What did it all mean? Tomorrow? Doña Sol? What will happen tomorrow?'

All night long I watched women squatting on the ground beneath me, working on a large piece of orange-coloured fabric, the shape of which I couldn't make out. They spoke about 'tomorrow', but all I caught were snippets of their conversation, which only piqued my curiosity without satisfying it.

Finally day broke: it was again a Tuesday. I had dozed off somewhere towards morning. Men coming to collect the orange fabric rudely awoke me, and one of them, taking off his jacket, threw it on me. I could no longer see anything. I could hear them coming and going, but I couldn't understand what was going on. I suffered greatly. The owner of the jacket returned, perspiring heavily, to collect his clothes. I opened my straws wide.

Oh, surprise! I see a great round, soft thing, the shape of an immense mushroom. It springs from the ground, stretching and widening out towards the sky, and the mushroom swells upwards, ever upwards!

Finally it rises from the ground, held down by some ropes. It's a balloon, a tiny orange balloon. It curtsies to the huge balloon, which wobbles like an elephant.

The crowd gathers; the balloon is entirely inflated. I catch sight of Doña Sol in the crowd. Louis Godard comes to look for me, and I go through the crowd in his arms, a little moved, greeting everyone who looks at me.

I am placed in a little basket for dirty laundry, and above my head is the small balloon, which now seems enormous. The crowd parts, and I think there must be another chair coming to keep me company… No! It is Doña Sol, leaning on the arm of Monsieur Gaston Tissandier. She is followed by the young painter, Georges Clairin. Monsieur D'Artois and the two celebrated Godards look into the basket to see if I am level and that nothing is bothering me. I was about to thank them for their care when I was blinded by a billow of lace.

Doña Sol was seated upon me!

Georges Clairin jumped into the basket, as did the young Louis Godard, nephew of the other two.

It was then half-past five. The crowd pressed closer and closer to the balloon, hats were raised, hands squeezed, farewells exchanged, and the balloon rapidly ascended, to great applause.

And then nothing! Nothing! The earth beneath, the sky above – I am in the clouds. I have left hazy Paris behind, and have found a blue sky and a radiant sun. The little basket plunges into a milky vapour warmed by the sun. All around us there are opaque mountains, with little iridescent crests, and a little lead-coloured line pushing away the background. It's admirable! It's amazing!

Not a sound, not a breath. It is not silence; it is the shadow of silence. It is soft, dimmed.

I hear Doña Sol murmur: 'If only I could always live like this.'

But all of a sudden the scene changes: the clouds separate, and the balloon begins to descend just above the Pont de la Concorde,* about a hundred metres from where we set off.

The crowd, which is still gathered in the courtyard of the Tuileries, rushes towards the quays. We seem to be plunging towards the Seine.

Clairin turns towards the aeronaut, a question on the tip of his tongue.

'I'm playing a joke on them,' said Louis Godard. 'You'll see.' And immediately he empties a bag of ballast, and we ascend once more to heaven.

There was absolutely no wind at all in the upper regions, and the balloon descended again just above the captive balloon.

But at last, at about six o'clock, the air currents increased, and we took flight in earnest to the east.

'Let's tidy up the balloon a little,' said Louis Godard, 'and make ourselves more comfortable.'

Straight away the ballast bags are moved from the bottom of the basket and placed outside. Doña Sol's mantle and her companion's waterproof are arranged above our heads in artistic folds, producing the most beautiful effect. The young woman had brought a pair of patent leather boots, which were hung outside the little basket; it seemed to annoy them greatly, because I heard the right boot whisper to the left, 'Frankly, she should have left us at home. If she wants to risk our necks on horseback, all right – but in a balloon…'

I was straining my ears to catch the rest of the sentence when my attention was seized and held by Doña Sol's golden voice.

'Ah! It annoys me,' she said, 'that chair! Suppose we throw it away?'

'Ah, but no, but no! You might kill a Parisian,' cried Georges Clairin. And he tore me from the hands of that madwoman, who had already seized me and was swinging me in space.

How dreadful!

I had heard, of course, that she burns cats in order to eat the roasted fur; that she makes delicacies from lizards' tails and peacocks' brains, sautéed in monkey-butter. I knew that she played croquet with skulls wearing Louis XIV wigs.* I believe her capable of anything, but oh! To massacre a poor chair that can do nothing to help itself – that surpasses anything I could have imagined.

My fate was hotly debated, and I was trembling with all my sticks when the younger Godard suddenly picked me up.

'Ah! bah! Madame is quite right, it does bother us — I'll fix that.'

I lost consciousness.

When I came to, I found myself hanging beside the little boots. I was swimming in space, secured to the basket only by a piece of string wrapped around my head. I had had a few moments of vertigo, then, slowly getting to grips with my new position, I began to take stock of where I was.

To my left, suspended by his handle, a small pot-bellied hamper was swinging. The basket resembled a second-hand shop on holiday. We were once more in the clouds, at an altitude of 1,600 metres.

The scenery was no less beautiful than on the first occasion. The grey clouds, fleecy as a swan's neck, served as a carpet. The great orange draperies, fringed with violet, hung down from the sun and were lost in a white and mossy lace. The balloon seemed not to move at all; it was cool, but not cold. The air was pure.

Doña Sol recited a beautiful lament.

'But that sounds just like Musset's Minuccio lament,'* said Georges Clairin.

'No, it is Musset's which sounds like Boccaccio's lament – or, to be more just, the poet translated it from the old French, verse by verse. Only, I prefer Boccaccio's.'

And the young woman recited this lament for the second time, which I remember. Here she is:

> Go tell him, Love, how much I suffer,
>   Tell to the Lord I soon shall expire,
> If soon He comes not to grant me succour,
>   Being too timid to tell my desire!
>
> Mercy, Love, with clasped hands I fervently say,
>   Call on my Lord at the place where He dwells,
> Tell Him how truly I desire and pray,
>   With so great ardour it must be I die!
> All full of passion I know not the hour
>   When I shall 'scape from so grievous a pain,
> If soon His pity comes not to succour
> I see no way by which peace to obtain.
> Thus shall I finish my life all too brief,
> Love to Him make known, alas, all my grief!
>
> E'er since my Lord I have so much beloved,
>   Neither of courage nor heart have I still,
> Like as of fear, alas, timorous soul!

>    Only from Him have I courage or will.
> Although my trouble is great, I confess,
>    All thought of death is oppression so great,
> And if I thought He would feel any distress
>    Should I my troubles to Him all relate,
> To him to tell it I feel powerless.
> To him, alas! Love, make known my distress!
>
> Since then, O Love, of hope I have none,
>    That my dear Lord can thus ever know,
> By any means, or appearance alone,
>    That which I suffer from sorrow and woe.
> Thee it may please Him to grant me but this,
>    That He remembers at least of that day
> When all the shock of that dark cruel dart,
>    Doing so well at the tourney its play
> Was by my glance turned aside from His heart.
> Yet, my Lord, I cannot bear my heart!*

And they struck up a literary conversation. Meanwhile, young Godard continued to manage the balloon.

A distant noise resembling the crumpling of paper attracted the attention of the travellers. A black whirlwind passed before us, then came back again above the balloon. It was a flight of swallows, already deserting our climate; perhaps a troop of little patients.*

In the midst of them, an old lady, completely dressed in black, with white lace upon her head, a serious air and the embonpoint of an old dowager. The whole band came to a halt, uttering piercing cries at the sight of the balloon. The old lady held a council of war, then the little savages flew twice around the balloon, screeching all the time, and then the whole band disappeared on swift wings.

The air had now become lukewarm, and the noises of the city came up to us, borne along on its dull fumes. Paris appeared underneath us again; we were above the Bastille. The humidity of the air had laden down our balloon, and we were going back down.

We had to throw out some more ballast. Doña Sol claimed the pleasure of opening the sack and covering the impudent genius of Liberty* with sand. An English family, taking the air on the balcony of the July Column, was blinded by our ballast. The father looked up angrily at the elegant genius, believing it to be a prank on his part. But the latter, his leg in the air, his arm crooked upward, continued his graceful posing with a suitably French nonchalance.

The sack emptied, ascended again rapidly; then, having encountered a swifter air current, the balloon began to move along with relative speed, but which to us seemed to us extreme, considering how slowly we had travelled until now.

The city rolled away beneath us, shaded by the approaching dusk. The streets seemed to me to be long adders, the boulevards immense boas at rest. La Villette, in the distance, with its immense gas bells,* looked like a calcined cemetery. The balloon stopped moving for a moment, hovering over a bizarre monument. It looked a bit like a gigantic wheel. Clairin, looking through a spyglass, recognised La Roquette.* It was the exercise hour. All the poor devils were watching the balloon, this son of the skies, emblem of absolute freedom. Their eyes were fixed upon the balloon, their arms dangling. Doña Sol looked through the spyglass, and gave voice to the various sensations that assaulted her. One of the condemned, walking in a narrow courtyard, leant against the wall and began to cry. Who knows – perhaps he was waiting for death, he who saw life, the sun, liberty overhead!

We resumed our flight towards the heavens. The travellers were a little sad. The wind driving us, we passed over the Père Lachaise Cemetery. Georges Clairin and Doña Sol saluted in passing the tombs of their friends; the young woman stripped the leaves from her corsage, and the white petals fell at random across the field of rest.

A large white veil majestically enveloped the cemetery. The balloon entered the folds of this veil, and moved on again, making little circuits. Twenty minutes after, emerging from limbo, we perceived Vincennes.*

It was half-past six, and those in the basket were hungry. As a wooden chair, my stomach demanded nothing; but the three travellers were not of the same constitution. They unhooked the little pot-bellied hamper. Doña Sol sat down at the back of the basket, and prepared toast with foie gras. Louis Godard, standing up, a bottle of champagne in his hand, made the cork fly out, which was lost in the ethereal regions. The detonation echoed from cloud to cloud; a frothy jet escaped from the bottle; a wisp of cloud passed and drank long draughts of the white foam, and went away to carry the drunkenness into the heavens. Then all the clouds began to flutter, kissing, striking, breaking one another and entirely enveloping us in their heavenly intoxication. Georges Clairin, pencil in hand, fixed in his album the strange scene of this dinner at 2,300 metres in the air. Doña Sol had set places, each with a tiny napkin, a slice of toast with foie gras and a glass. The young woman had a little silver goblet.

The sky was beautiful, and the weather had put on its brightest robe. The dinner passed very cheerfully; two courses were served: first was the toast with foie gras, and second was slices of foie gras. Then a delicious dessert of oranges, and that was it. We toasted Monsieur

Giffard, the future of balloons, fame, the arts, to 'that which was, is and shall be'; then the bottle, thrown up in the air, fell waltzing into the lake of Vincennes. The swans, startled, beat their wings, and the lake frowned; then, the bottle having vanished, there was a calm.

There was a moment of vague sadness.

'Poor bottle,' murmured Doña Sol. 'It reminds me of an old actress. Sparkling and heady, she has given us her all; and, ungrateful and weary of her, we throw her away, without regret, into eternal oblivion.'

'Ah! bah! Live your life, since death is at the end!' cried Georges Clairin.

'Ah, but you are not gay,' remarked Louis Godard. 'Sad thoughts are not welcome on this trip – you will weigh down the balloon, and we shall descend. Ballast, ballast... To the Devil with your philosophical thoughts!'

The travellers, laughing at this joke, opened the cage of the black butterflies.\* We had to empty a new sack. Ill luck willed it that the ballast fell in its entirety upon a wedding party that was stretched out on the grass below. We had descended with such rapidity that we were no more than 500 metres above the ground. The shower of pebbles was greeted with a shout of horror. Immediately the furious bride turned towards a little boy of seven or eight who was peaceably playing at horse

astride an umbrella, and gave him a vigorous wallop. We had taken out our spyglasses, and Doña Sol, piqued by this injustice, threw the tin box which had held the foie gras at the wedding party. They all looked up. The balloon was prevented from rising, the valve being half-open, the travellers not wishing to miss any of this delicious scene. Hands cupped, the wedding party were screaming curses, which unfortunately did not reach the balloon. The child that had been smacked in error was trying to throw stones at us, but a packet of sweets thrown to him by the young woman stopped him, and he sat down peacefully to count his wealth.

The groom, who had never ceased ranting, was suddenly seized by an idea, and disappeared behind a bush; there, thinking himself well concealed, since he couldn't see us, took off his coat, then his waistcoat, then his braces... seeing which, Doña Sol asked to ascend to the heavens once more, fearing it was indiscreet to remain. But no – it was a false alarm. He took one of his braces, picked up a stone and readied his slingshot for use against the balloon; he stood up, steadies himself and – one – two – three – he collapses prostrate into a huge puddle.

The whole wedding party was seized with laughter: we watched in rapture the children's antics, the mother-in-law in hysterics, her belly, chest and legs writhing in dreadful

# IN THE CLOUDS

convulsions, the young bride holding her sides – and our basket leapt right and left with the intensity of the laughter of the three travellers, and the hanging boots bashed against one other, cracking their polish off.

I rolled against the pot-bellied hamper, which rolled back against me. Finally the clouds, already grey, burst into laughter, and the comedy ends in a downpour.

## IN THE CLOUDS

Our balloon sheltering us from the deluge, we passed through the rain without getting wet. We rose above the clouds and reached the sun, leaving the earth under a veil of rain.

Again we saw a remarkable spectacle. The sun, furious at having to go to bed so soon, was red with anger; small grey clouds, teasing him, passed and repassed incessantly before him. He looked like a wounded lion tormented by flies.

The horizon was marked by great black lines; the clouds are opaque about us.

'You might think yourself at sea on a foggy day,' Clairin observed.

The storm rumbles slyly in the distance. We are at 2,400 metres above sea level. It's almost hot. We leave Joinville-le-Pont* behind us; the Marne* rolls itself along like a satin ribbon; the little boats seem like fish on the surface of the water; the view is entrancing. It is the twilight hour. Everything takes a balmy air of poetry.

We travel onwards; we travel quickly, crossing plains and woods, passing over smiles and tears. Here is a cheerful garden; they sing, they laugh around the table. Here is a little cemetery; a woman is weeping. All kinds of life unfolds beneath us, from house to house. The balloon passes over a grand park; there is a party at the château. They go, they come, they dance.

'Oh! How small men seem from such a height! And the good Lord, who even higher! But He mustn't see anything from there.'

As I made this reflection, one of the boots gave me a kick. I returned to my straws.

The sun had decidedly set. It was a quarter past seven. Night covered her shoulders with her brown mantle. The balloon was at an altitude of 2,600 metres. It was the highest we had yet ascended. The earth had completely disappeared. A poesy, somewhat sad, enveloped us.

Doña Sol and Georges Clairin sang a Breton ballad. I was starting to go to sleep, letting myself drift into sweet drowsiness, when Louis Godard's voice made me start.

'Come! Come! We must think of descending. Cast out the guide rope!'

'What! Already?' cried the travellers. 'What a pity!'

'Oh, yes! Yes, it's getting late. It's a question of descending in a skilful way. To the guide rope!' he said, untangling a rope.

'To the guide rope! To the guide rope!' repeated the two young people.

I looked to see what this guide rope might be, and I saw him unroll a long rope, on which little iron grapnels were attached at regular intervals.

The young painter and actress bravely set to work assisting the aeronaut. The rope was 120 metres long. Godard, leaning out of the basket, watched it unroll, while Clairin and Doña Sol played it out gently through their hands, stopping it from dropping too fast, laughing when one or the other was scratched by the hooks. Finally, the rope unwound, Godard took out his spyglass.

'The Devil! There are so many trees,' he murmured.

Indeed, at this moment the balloon was just over a little wood; ahead was a plain, and then woods as far as the eye could see. After orienting himself, the aeronaut declared it absolutely imperative to descend into the plain, or we risked making a descent into the Ferrières Forest* in the middle of the night. It was now or never. Doña Sol had the great pleasure of opening the valve to its full extent. Gas escaped, mocking, hissing. Then, the valve closed again, we descended quite rapidly. When we were at about 500 metres, Louis Godard took from one of his pockets (veritable stockpiles) a little trumpet, and blew through it with violence.

'O, God!' I'm missing my cue!'* cried Doña Sol. And, losing her head, she was about to rush out into space; but Clairin caught her.

'Calm yourself,' he said to her. 'It is not Hernani calling, it's the stationmaster!'*

All three burst into laughter. In fact, while all this was going on we had crossed a little hamlet, just on the edge of the woods, and we found ourselves hovering over the eastern line.

It was a curious sight: the black railway lines winding in all directions, their steel cords lit up. Silence reigned everywhere, and then, all of a sudden, a formidable monster was seen approaching at full speed, two eyes blazing with anger, spitting flames from its iron jaws and forming battalions of clouds with its hot breath, which rose boldly towards the sky.

The stationmaster, seeing a balloon and understanding how late it was for a landing, called his men to prepare to lend their assistance, in case it was required.

'Where are we?' cried Louis Godard through the trumpet.

'A-u-u-u-ille,' responded the stationmaster.

Impossible to understand.

'Where are we?' cried Clairin in his turn, in a terrible voice.

'A-u-u-u-ille,' shouted back the stationmaster, cupping his hands.

'Where are we?' sang Doña Sol's shrill voice.

'A-u-u-u-ille,' responded the whole band.

# IN THE CLOUDS

Nothing. Nothing!

We needed to lose more ballast. We were descending too quickly, and the wind was dragging us back into the woods we had just left.

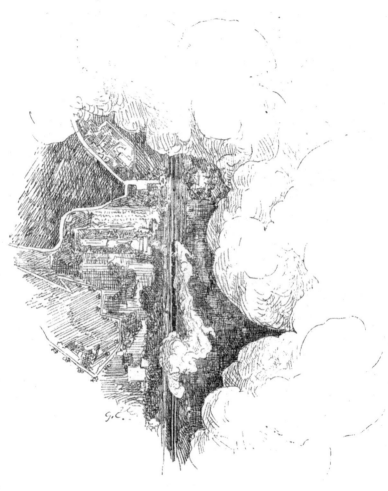

The night was advancing. We ascended again towards the sky. It was dark blue, all dotted with grey clouds. After ten minutes on the way, the valve was opened again, and we began to descend. The balloon was to the right of the station, very far from its obliging master.

'The anchor, now!' said young Godard; and a new rope was flung out. At the end was fastened a formidable anchor. The rope measured eighty metres. Noises came to us from the ground, confused, but sharp. I couldn't understand what it was I saw swarming below me.

'Ah! My God! What a troop of children!' cried Doña Sol.

Indeed, we were followed by children, who, scrambling over hedges, crossing the fields, were running after the balloon, ever since its halt over the railway station.

We were only 300 metres from the earth.

The trumpet performed its office: 'Where are we?'

'Verchères,'* cried the merry band. (They had to be made to repeat this many times.)

'Where is this Verchères?' asked Clairin.

'I don't know.'

'Nor I.'

'Bah! We shall soon see.'

The balloon was still descending, but very slowly now.

The aeronaut cast out the ballast, then opened the valve; all in all, the descent was done in quite a remarkable way; and, although the opinion of a wooden chair probably matters little to him, I offer him my compliments, all the same.

The peasants had come running. The night obscured the landscape, and everything took on a more dramatic aspect.

'Come on, all you over there, grab hold of that dangling rope – and be careful not to pull too hard.'

At this moment I caught sight of the balloon, and was stunned. What was earlier so round was now flat, wrinkled, the hem of its skirts swinging over the basket. Oh, it was miserable!

The peasants had seized the rope, and were about to pull on it when the aeronaut shouted to them to stop.

'Ah! Let's not fall into the pond!'

Indeed, just beneath us a little pond threatened us with a ducking; in a few minutes we had passed by it.

'Come, now, children: to the rope, and gently!'

Five vigorous men took the long rope. We were 120 metres from the ground, and I assure you that, for a chair that had never before travelled, it was a very strange sight. The night now enveloped us. Nothing preserved its true aspect. The peasants seemed to us to be giants; the children were Lilliputians. Women had

also arrived, and, in the midst of those heads, some bare, some covered with silk handkerchiefs or with caps, three bowler hats flourished in their self-importance as landowners' headwear.

Young Godard was giving orders, looking to the right, to the left, everywhere; encouraging the workmen: 'Bravo, friends – perfectly – slowly. Behave yourselves like French knights; there's a lady in the basket.'

'A lady!' cried the peasants in chorus.

'A lady!' repeated the echo.

'A lady!' croaked the frogs in the pond.

And the crowd rushed towards the balloon. A Curious, less patient than the others, struck a match. The young aeronaut gave a roar of anger.

'Well! My good man, if you have another, why not light that too, and come and blow us all up!'

This was greeted with a general cry, and the imprudent Curious was cursed at, jostled and pushed back into the crowd.

The crowd had pulled back in terror, and if it wasn't for our anchor, which was firmly stuck in the ground, we should have departed for the heavens. Finally, curiosity overcoming their fear, they returned en masse.

'Take the ropes, and stand on tiptoe, mademoiselle,' said Godard to the actress. 'Above all, have no fear: I will bring you to land without a shock.'

He kept his word. Thanks to his skilful manoeuvres, the basket landed just like a bird. I was afraid of breaking my four wooden legs on striking the ground, but that wasn't the case. I remained suspended from the basket without feeling the slightest oscillation.

'There's the lady! There's the lady!' cried the children.

'Let's see who she is!' said the women.

A child saw me.

'Ah! A chair hanging upside down from the balloon. What a funny idea, a balloon chair!'

'It's for balance,' said a bowler hat.

Georges Clairin jumped to the ground, and made to lift out Doña Sol.

'No, no, no, I don't want to get out... I was promised a little drag – I want my little drag.'

'Ah! That will have to wait for next time, madame. The elements are against you. Today we must accept this banal descent.'

Doña Sol allowed herself to be lifted out, sighing; the painter placed her gently on the ground, and the crowd immediately surrounded her.

'Ah, madame!' said one young girl, touching her dress.

'Ah! Holy Mary! I myself would never risk my skin in such a machine as that,' said an old, wrinkled, bent and blackened-with-age peasant woman, crossing herself.

'That would be a pity, Mother; the country would lose its most beautiful ornament, and Monsieur le Curé his youngest lamb.'

The little group roared with laughter.

Doña Sol's place in the basket had been taken by a tall fellow – it was the same with each traveller – but really, it was quite unnecessary for the young woman to get out, for she lightened the balloon when in it even more than she loaded it. The three peasants holding on to the ropes were lifted to the height of a few metres from the ground, to the great delight of the lookers-on. The boots, the basket and I were still hanging. Finally the balloon touched down definitively. Georges Clairin came to untie me, and carried me into the field. Doña Sol seated herself upon me and put on her little boots. The ground was soaked, and the freshly cut hay wafted its sweet perfume.

The three bowler hats approached, talking quietly.

'I assure you it's her,' said a young, fresh voice.

'No, no,' replied a stiff voice.

'Perhaps,' the third hat whispered.

'I recognised her voice.'

And the young man, approaching the young woman, greeted her, saying: 'It is a great honour for our modest village, mademoiselle, to host Doña Sol.'

'So you recognise me, monsieur? How's that? You can scarcely see me.'

'By your voice, mademoiselle.'

'Ah, really? That gives me great pleasure, and I am very flattered, monsieur.'

The second hat approached: 'I have the right to hold a grudge against mademoiselle.'

'And why is that, monsieur?'

'Because you refused the invitation I had the honour to offer you.'

'Ah! But I don't understand at all…'

'Me neither,' added the youngest.

'Nor I.'

'Nor I.'

'It is quite simple, nevertheless; what happened was the balloon passed over my property about an hour ago – for I am a landowner, mademoiselle, the largest landholder in the country. I had people over for dinner; we went out to see the balloon, and I recognised mademoiselle at once.'

The young woman stifled her laughter.

'Ah! bah!' said Clairin, mockingly. 'Then it was you, monsieur, who gestured to us? Ah! I remember you very well – oh! Very well!'

'See,' said the landowner, beaming at the two other hats in amazement.

Thanks to the darkness, everyone was hidden, and he was able to continue.

'So I recognised Mademoiselle Doña Sol, and I gestured, as Monsieur Godard just said – whom I also recognised.'

'Ah! Me too, monsieur?' murmured Clairin.

'Yes, Monsieur Godard, immediately! So I gestured to you, and I hoped that the balloon would descend into my park, and that I should have the honour of having you at my table. But someone in the basket shouted an inconceivable 'Peewit!',\* and the balloon moved off. There you have it, mademoiselle – that's why I have a right to bear you a slight grudge.'

This was all said in a starched manner, with a deep, nasal accent. In fine, he seemed to be an absolute copy of the famous actor, Baron.* At this moment young Godard joined us, and, fearing that he might spoil everything, Doña Sol exclaimed, introducing him: 'This is Monsieur Clairin, our travelling companion.'

'Ah, of course! Monsieur the Director wouldn't allow his shareholder to run all the risks of air travel alone. Well! Monsieur *Perrin*,* I offer you my compliments.'

Young Godard, catching on, was about to respond; but, fearing he should betray himself, he leapt off like a goat over a hillock, calling out: 'Come, children, to the balloon! We need to deflate the balloon.'

'He is very gay, Monsieur Perrin,' said the false Baron. 'Very gay, and very young. He must be beloved.'

'Oh yes, monsieur, absolutely beloved.'

A general outcry arrested this bizarre conversation. The sky had just opened up all its sluices. In an instant we were absolutely overcome. I sank into the earth. Doña Sol got up, and, wrapping herself in furs, remained standing.

'But you'll be drenched, mademoiselle,' said the sorry young man.

'Oh! Fear not, monsieur. I am so thin I can pass between the raindrops!'

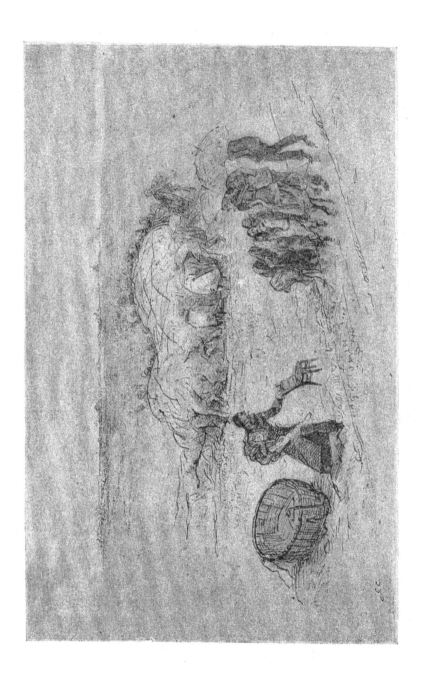

The women and children, covered only by their camisoles, put their petticoats over their heads. A little girl of ten or twelve, forgetting that she had only her petticoat to cover her, remained bare from the waist down, and despite the attention paid to her, she persisted, hoping that no one could see clearly.

All of the children had gathered around the young woman, who sheltered three of them under her large coat. Georges Clairin and Godard worked on the balloon, with the help of about twenty men.

It was a bizarre spectacle. The field in which we were standing being very large, the horizon appeared to us very distant. The balloon, lying on the ground, was breathing heavily. The men pressed its sides and gas escaped like a powerful breath – one might say it was like a gigantic grumbling turtle. The mesh of the net, obscured by the dark of the night, completed the illusion by forming the scales of the beast. The men were soaked with perspiration and rain. Doña Sol was very touched by the attention of a little boy, who had gone to hunt for an umbrella for her; she used it to shelter a few children, and especially the considerate little boy, who was now sweating profusely.

'People are very gallant in this little place,' she said, smiling.

At this point, the third hat, approaching, made his voice heard. (He was the one who had only said 'Perhaps.') But, happy to finally introduce himself, he sang in a soft and slow voice: 'Yes, mademoiselle, you are quite right. This land is the very centre of simple and amiable customs. All these good people love and sustain one another. Thus this little one, whom you caress so kindly, he is an orphan. But all the peasants are to him as father and mother, and the shepherd has taken him in.'

'And you, monsieur?'

'I encourage them, mademoiselle. I am the oldest landowner in the country; they are all my children, and this commune will be rich after my death.'

'But monsieur, I am not an orphan – Papa is not dead.'

'No, my little man, no – but it isn't far off, because your dear father will be guillotined.'

I jumped in terror. Doña Sol supressed a movement of fear; the child began to cry; and the third hat, happy with the effect produced, continued his monotonous chant: 'Alas! Yes, it is a very sad story. The dear father of this child killed his good mother about a month ago. Hold on, mademoiselle, for the rest! The crime was committed right where that chair now stands.'

I jumped in fear; the half-orphan who had clambered up on me was thrown to the ground.

'Ah! Here, here – how very funny… What's the chance? The child has fallen right there! Yes, it is on that very spot that the unfortunate woman was murdered.'

'And how?' demanded Doña Sol, after picking up the child.

'Oh! It's very simple, mademoiselle. These young people no longer loved one another. The husband, especially, wanted to take another wife. It's possible if one is single, like me; but marriage is absolute, and in the countryside one isn't rich enough to get a separation.'* In short, one morning when the poor woman had come to bring her husband his lunch, as he was cutting the very hay of which you see the stubble, the latter struck her with his scythe; but that only damaged her leg. Neither of them said a word about it. Some time later they returned to load up some bundles of hay that had to be taken back. The woman was standing there by the wagon, and he threw the bundles to her from over yonder. At the fifth he shouted to her, "Here, Mother, take care of that!" and he threw the pitchfork at her, which stuck in the neck of the unfortunate woman. It was the shepherd, hidden in that little wood, who saw and related the story.'

While this sad tale was being told, the women gradually retreated from the scene of the crime. The dismayed children listened to the drawling voice chanting the sad odyssey. The balloon itself assumed a dramatic air. Pressed by the strong hands of the peasants, it had become flattened, crushed; a few last breaths rasped from its mutilated body, its chest heaving violently. Eventually, however, it grew drowsy, and took on the appearance of a boa in repose. The rain continued to fall. Doña Sol enquired by what train we might be able to return.

'Oh! Only by the 10 o'clock train, because the railway station is an hour from here by carriage; and, since there are none here, it will take two hours on foot, walking swiftly.'

'But that's impossible!' cried Clairin. 'Mademoiselle will never be able to walk that far.'

'There must be another way,' said the actress.

And, looking around for the young man – the first hat – she seemed disappointed not to see him.

'Ah! He has gone to bed, that young farmer,' said the gruff voice. 'In my day one was more gallant.'

'We're just as gallant, but more practical, dear sir,' said the young accused, jumping nimbly from a carriage which had just arrived without our hearing it. 'I've just come from my house, where I have hitched up two carriages – one for mademoiselle and her companions, the other for the remains of the balloon.'

Doña Sol held out her hand to the young man, thanking him.

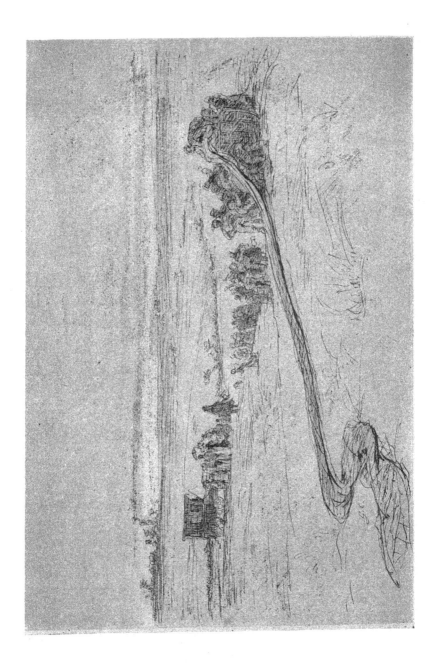

'By my faith! You have saved us!' said Georges Clairin. 'It seems the roads are not easy.'

'Oh! It would have been impossible for the feet of a Parisienne to travel even half the distance!'

During this little episode, Godard had rolled up the balloon and had put it in the basket with its guide rope, its anchor and its ropes. The second carriage having arrived, the balloon was hauled into it with difficulty. Poor balloon! So gay, so dapper a few hours ago, it was now all crumpled, all trampled down in the bottom of its basket. Its beautiful orange colour had washed away in the stormy, fierce rain. Everybody was silent. It was a funeral service.

Then Louis Godard, putting on a solemn air, said: 'Listen, all, to me!'

We approached him.

'Here is a little something Doña Sol and Georges Clairin ask you to accept, that you might drink the health of Monsieur Giffard.'

Men, women, children rushed upon the young captain.

'To me! To me, monsieur!'

And hands are stretched out.

'Who is the oldest among you?'

'It's me, monsieur!'

'No, it's me!'

A little longer and the children would have sworn that they were eighty years old.

'Give it to me,' said a scary-looking short man. 'I will treat them all tonight, and tomorrow we'll make lunch from the leftovers.'

It was the owner of the only restaurant in the village* who spoke thus. The proposal was accepted, and the money was placed in his hands.

Then the little troop wished us a safe journey, and they all disappeared across the fields; they looked a bit like a cloud of sparrows that had been dispersed by someone throwing stones at them.

Everyone had approached the road, and I was left alone in the killing field. Doña Sol was getting into the vehicle, when, turning around all of a sudden, she said: 'My chair! Where is my chair? I want it.'

'Bah! Tomorrow it will make some peasant happy. Leave it there,' said Louis Godard.

'No! No! I love it, that chair; bring it to me.'

The joy I felt set my heart racing, and although I couldn't understand this sudden tenderness, I forgot my grievances and began to love her again. Clairin looked for me for a few minutes, and then carried me to the carriage, placing me near the young woman.

'Poor chair! How soaked it is!' she said, wiping away both the raindrops and my tears; for I was crying like an animal, I was so nervous.

The carriage I found myself in was an elegant one.*

Doña Sol was sat in the back; by her side was Clairin, opposite me, lying on one of the seats. In the corner Louis Godard, tired, stood opposite the gruff voice. The third hat had gone ahead on foot. The young man in the seat drove, and had at his side our blankets, the pot-bellied hamper and the orphan, who we were going to leave at the shepherd's house as we passed. The grey mare set off at good speed, leaving the carriage carrying the defunct balloon far behind.

The conversation was languishing. The rain continued to fall; the roads were very bad; the night was pitch black; not one house was lit up. It was cold, and everyone was hungry, it seems. Everybody was starting to doze off, when the carriage suddenly stopped, and the young farmer spoke to Doña Sol:

'Mademoiselle, do you see that little hut hidden under those birch trees? It is inhabited by a poor madwoman, who is very interesting. Twenty-two years ago, she lost her seven-year-old son, who was nicknamed 'The Nightingale', he sang so beautifully. The unhappy mother, since then, spends her days – winter and summer, rain, frost or scorching sun – searching for worms, caterpillars and ants, with which she fills her hut, and at night she walks around, calling to her son and sowing her strange crop as she goes. Listen!' he said.

A sad, quavering voice rose in the gloom of the night: 'Nightingale! Nightingale! Nightingale! Come, little one!'

A shadow came out of the thicket, followed the hedge and entered a field, tracing its broad, curved line against the horizon. The half-bare shoulders were stung by the rain; the arms swung in cadence, sowing her seed of caterpillars and ants, and then the shadow disappeared into the night. 'Nightingale! Nightingale!' the voice continued to moan. Then there was silence.

'Poor, poor mother!' whispered the actress. She wiped away a tear with the tip of her gloved finger, and the carriage went on again, bouncing and happy.

We were entering the village.

The carriage stopped in front of a gate, and the man with the gruff voice got out.

'This is my home. I wish you a good trip, mademoiselle. Monsieur Perrin, Monsieur Godard, I salute you.' And he gravely entered his park. We continued our journey. Stop! We are finally at the station. Everyone gets out; the young woman takes me under her arm and we enter.

'Here, Monsieur Godard!' cries the stationmaster. 'Ah, Mademoiselle Doña Sol!'

'Do you know us all, then?' asked Clairin.

'Ah! Monsieur, I adore balloons, and I love the theatre. But come into my office – it's warmer than here, and mademoiselle must be freezing.'

The amiable man installed us in his office.

'Where are we?'

'At Émerainville...* It was you I saw at about seven o'clock, wasn't it? I thought you would descend here.'

'Ah! bah! Was it you that we asked—'

'Yes – yes – the place. I shouted it to you as loud as I could, but I could tell you didn't hear. Ah! Monsieur is an artist?' he said, on seeing Clairin sketching.

'Yes, I'm a painter.'

'Oh! What a joy for me to play host to an artist! I adore them, monsieur, I adore them!'

'Is there any chance of getting something to eat, and a glass of water? I'm dying of hunger and thirst,' said Godard.

'Is that so? I can sort that out for you.'

A few moments later a child brought bread, cheese and cider.

'Ah! But I don't like cheese, myself,' objected Doña Sol.

'Bah! For once you will like it,' replied Clairin.

'But it smells bad…'

'No! Let's be rustic, dear madame – no one is looking at you.'

The young woman gave her companion a playful tap, and bravely started to eat the bread and cheese.

During this rather frugal meal, the owner of the carriages oversaw the unloading of the balloon. The basket, filled with the remains of the balloon, was taken out and put in the storeroom. Poor son of the skies! Prisoner in a cage, and stamped all over with baggage marks.\*

The train was very late; but the stationmaster told us that was the fault of the plums. Why? Mystery! Finally the whistle was heard; we rushed out onto the platform – I was still being carried by Doña Sol. We thanked the stationmaster for his hospitality. M. Clairin gave his card to the young farmer, who gave his own in exchange, and, Doña Sol, approaching Monsieur B——, extended her gratitude for all the services he had rendered, and the good grace with which he had done so.

We get into the train. Doña Sol puts her feet on me: I kiss them gratefully. Clairin lies down opposite us on a bench, and Louis Godard makes himself comfortable. The train leaves; everyone goes to sleep; and, as for myself, I try my best to make sense of my

thoughts, which are troubled by so many diverse adventures. Only yesterday I was a dreaming chair, regarding as impossibilities a carpet, a living room, a carriage, a little trip; but since yesterday I have spent a night in a fantastic hangar; I have passed through a large crowd who warmly greeted me; I have gone up in a balloon; I have rested for an hour in a field that has witnessed a horrible crime; I have travelled in a carriage; I have seen a madwoman; finally, I'm riding along the railway!!! Whatever will happen to me next? O, Virgin of the Chair, protect me!

I fall asleep: how long did my slumber last? I do not know. Here we are in Paris. The travellers get out; each takes a package; Doña Sol takes me in her arms. My temples throb like crazy: I am scared! Very scared! We stop two carriages. The actress gets into one of them with me alone.

'As for you,' she said to Clairin and Godard, 'go and assure our friends of our safety, and goodnight!'

In fact, MM. Giffard, Tissandier and Godard had made the travellers promise to let them know the result of the descent as soon as possible. As the telegraph only works until nine o'clock in the wild regions surrounding Paris, they had had no news. But the young men fulfilled their promise, and went off gaily, despite the late hour and their great fatigue.

Here I am in the vehicle with my friend: we are leaving! Where am I going...? Where am I going...? We travel for half an hour, and the vehicle goes along a grand tree-lined avenue. The young woman leans over, stops the coachman brusquely, and tells him to continue at a walk. She laughs to herself, making little exclamations: 'Ah! Ah! Choked up? Him too, ah...! And him...! How about this one... and this other... but they are all crazy!'

I stood up so I could see. A shadow passed, glancing into the carriage. Doña Sol hid her head. Another shadow walks nervously to the right, striking the pavement with his cane; shadows, assembled at a distance, are in a cloud of despair.* We advance into the midst of the shadows. I'm afraid... I'm afraid! We are still advancing. Opposite is a brilliantly lit house, covered all over with ivy. On the terrace women, men, children and dogs gaze at the horizon. Doña Sol laughs herself into tears. The carriage turns: it stops at the gate of the brilliantly lit house. A frightful clamour rises into the night. Shadows rush and jostle... the terrace becomes deserted... women and children cry, dogs bark. The street is waking up; the peacekeeping inhabitants are worried.

'You haven't caught anything...? Are you all right...? You don't have a cold?'

A woman in her forties advances... she is very pale.

'You have tormented us very much, my dear child,' she said, in a soft and serious voice.

'Dear Madame Guérard, don't worry; I haven't been at all injured – and I had such a wonderful time,' said Doña Sol, embracing her affectionately. Then, disengaging herself from all these embraces, she begged them to let her get into her home.

'But drop that chair!' said a gentleman, trying to take me.

'No, no! Don't you touch my chair! No one can touch my chair! Here! Félicie, I entrust it to you,' she said to her young maid. The young woman to whom I was entrusted was a pretty brunette, witty and sweet, evidently the chief housekeeper. She carried me into a huge room, filled with rugs (my dream!), palm trees and all sorts of objects. Oh, how happy I was! I looked around, I looked around... but imagine my terror when I saw, perched upon a large vase, a stuffed white swan, then, in the vase, a grand palm tree, and on the branches of the palm two monkeys in the arms one another, the one white, the other black... then another monkey on another frond – this one was grey. I also saw a red-and-green bird with emerald wings, an enormous bat with a grimace, a cat skeleton, two parakeets, a heather cock and a large greyhound skeleton! What a show!

So here is the lair of the woman with the golden voice… here are her victims! I looked away in horror, but my gaze fell upon even more appalling objects. At the end of the room a small dark staircase descended – to hell, I thought; in the corner, attached by a ring, hung a skeleton – a human skeleton! This time anger took hold of me; I wanted to rush out and inform the authorities that a crime had been committed… What am I saying, one? Perhaps ten crimes… maybe more. With a sudden movement, I broke loose from Félicie's hands and rolled to the ground. At the sound of my fall Doña Sol came running in.

'Ah! My chair… my poor chair! I prized it so much; it has a broken foot… what a pity!'

I had, in fact, broken my leg. Pulling a satin bow from her dress, she mended me in an instant.

'What are you going to do with this chair, dear madame?' asked a friend.

'I am going to put it in my souvenir cabinet.'

I gazed at the mysterious staircase in dread.

'It is large, this cabinet?' enquired a grey-haired gentleman.

'Very large! And upon the door is written: "Everything passes, everything breaks, everything runs out."* And now, goodnight, gentlemen,' said Doña Sol, shaking hands with some, allowing others to kiss hers.

Everyone withdrew.

'Come, put me to bed, Félicie. Goodnight, my chair!'

The next day, at dawn, she came downstairs dressed like a boy, holding a little hammer in her hand. Behind her, her butler, husband of the pretty Félicie, carried a box of nails and a stack of little green boxes. She knelt in front of me, and, with a charming gentleness, she drove twenty-two gilt nails into my chest. On each of them she hung a medal, on which were engraved these words: 'Souvenir of my ascent in the great hot-air balloon of Monsieur Henry Giffard.'*

Ever since then I have stayed in my corner, a silent witness to many very curious things. My feet rest on an oriental rug; my polished straws shine brilliantly in the sunlight; my leg being broken and my decorated chest has given me the nickname of 'The Invalid'. I have everything that I dreamt of; I ought to be happy, and yet I can't help singing with Béranger: *

# IN THE CLOUDS

How much I regret
My *wood* not bent,
My leg well shaped,
And my time misspent!*

## NOTE ON THE TEXT AND ILLUSTRATIONS

This story was first published in French as *Dans les nuages: Impressions d'une chaise* in 1878. It was translated by John Joline Ross and published in the *Seaside Library* (Vol. 43, No. 874) in November 1880. The text of the Renard edition is based on Ross' translation, but has been adapted to make it more faithful to the original French and more suitable for the modern reader. Italicisation in the text demonstrating stress has been taken from Bernhardt's text. In French the narrative darts between tenses, and this has been preserved in the English, except for in instances that seem accidental or jarring. The illustrations in this edition replicate those printed in the original French edition (they were not printed in the *Seaside Library*), including their placement.

## NOTES

10 *furniture-movers' vans*: In Paris furniture is moved from houses for domestic or foreign transport in immense vans, veritable houses on wheels, drawn, generally, by four or more horses (TRANSLATOR'S NOTE).

11 *the Tuileries*: A former palace on the right bank of the Seine in Paris.

12 *Doña Sol*: Doña Sol is a thinly veiled representation of Bernhardt herself; the name is taken from a character in the 1830 play *Hernani* by Victor Hugo (1802–85). Set in the Spanish Court in 1519, three men all vie for the attentions of Doña Sol.

14 *That was clear, huh… pun*: In the French, 'clear, huh' ('*clair, hein*') is pronounced like 'Clairin', the illustrator of this book, who was rumoured to be Bernhardt's lover.

14 *It would scarcely support Doña Sol*: Bernhardt was known to be very thin.

17 *Louis Godard*: The French aeronaut who conducted the ascents of the *ballon-captif* for M. Giffard in Paris in 1878 and 1879 at Paris World's Fair.

20 *Pont de la Concorde*: A bridge in Paris, which connects the Quai des Tuileries at the Place de la Concorde and the Quai d'Orsay.

22 *Louis XIV wigs*: That is, wigs in the style of Louis XIV (1638–1715, r. 1643–1715): long, curled black hair.

24 *Musset's Minuccio lament*: A reference to '*Complainte de Minuccio*' by Alfred de Musset-Pathay (1810–57).

26 *Go tell him… heart*: The translation deviates here from the rhyme scheme of the original, and takes a few liberties with the French in order to recreate the reading experience. In Bernhardt's original:

> Va dire, Amour, ce qui me faict douloir,
> Compte au Seigneur que je m'en vois mourir
> S'il ne me vient ou me veult secourir,
> Celant par craincte un deaireux vouloir.

Mercy, Amour, à joinctes mains te crie,
Voy mon Seigneur au lien où il demeure,
Dy luy comment je le desire et prie,
Tant que d'ardeur il fauldra que je meure,
Toute enflambée et ne sçachant point l'heure
Que perdre puisse une peine si griefve,
Si sa pitié bien tost ne me relieve,
Je ne voy point moyen de me r'avoir.
Ains finira tantost ma vie briesve.
Helas, Amour, fay luy mon mal sçavoir.

Depuis que fuz de luy si amoreuse,
Je n'ay point eu le cueur ni l'avantage,
Comme la craincte, helas, pauvre paoureuse,
De luy compter mon vouloir et courage,
Dont d'ennuy suis en telle peine et rage,
Qu'ainsi mourant, mourir m'est grand oppresse,
Et si croy bien qu'il en auroit destresse,
Si bonnement ma peine il pouvoit voir;
De luy mander je n'ay la hardiesse.
Helas, Amour, fay luy mon mal sçavoir.

Puis doncq, Amour, que je n'ay l'esperance
Que mon Seigneur puisse sçavoir, helas,
Par nul moyen jamais, ne par semblance,
Ce que je seuffre en mon pauvre cueur las,
Il te plaira me donner ce soulas,
Qu'il lui souvienne au moins de la journée
Qu'il combattit à la lance mornée,
Faisant tant bien au tournoy son devoir,
Par mon regard fut lors si adjournée
Que je n'en puis faire mon mal sçavoir.

27 *a troop of little patients*: An allusion to ill people going south to warmer climes for winter.
28 *genius of Liberty*: The July Column (Colonne de Juillet) in the Place de la Bastille, celebrating the Second French Revolution of 1830, is topped with a gilt figure, the *Génie de la Liberté* (literally, 'genius of liberty', but known in English as the *Spirit of Freedom*).
31 '*La Villette…gas bells*': La Villette is a former suburb of Paris, where a great gasworks was located. The French refer to the great gasholders as '*cloches*' ('bells').
31 *La Roquette*: A former prison, situated in the Rue Roquette, near the main entrance of Père Lachaise Cemetery; viewed from above, the prison was in the shape of a hexagon, with spokes meeting at a central tower.
32 *Vincennes*: A suburb of Paris famous for its ancient fortress and dungeons.
33 *opened the cage of the black butterflies:* i.e. they cast out their philosophical (dark) thoughts.
37 *Joinville-le-Pont*: A commune in the south-eastern suburbs of Paris; the translator notes that it was 'much frequented in the summer by Parisian shopkeepers and clerks, who take their wives and sweethearts out there on a Sunday.'
37 *the Marne*: A tributary of the Seine.
40 *Ferrières Forest*: The Forêt de Ferrières, a vast forest some twenty miles east of Paris.
40 *O, God… missing my cue*: An allusion to a scene in *Hernani* (see note to p. 12) where Hernani calls Doña Sol to his side with his bugle.
43 *Calm yourself… stationmaster*: At the time a stationmaster would use a tin horn to warn the passengers of an approaching train.
45 *Verchères*: A small village near Paris (TRANSLATOR'S NOTE).

NOTES

- 52 *shouted an inconceivable 'Peewit!'*: The peewit (lapwing) is known for its loud, piercing cry.
- 53 *the famous actor, Baron*: Michel Baron (1653–1729) was a French actor and playwright, and was the protégé of Molière. He came to have the reputation of quite the auteur, in that he was the author, actor and hero of his 1686 play *L'homme à bonnes fortunes* (*The Man of Good Fortunes*).
- 53 *Monsieur the Director... Perrin*: The Perrin for whom Clairin is mistaken is Émile Perrin (1814–85), the director of the Comédie-Française, a Paris theatre founded in 1680, at which Bernhardt was a leading star. Bernhardt was a *sociétaire* (a leading actor, normally a shareholder, at the theatrical company of the Comédie-Française), having been an acting member of the troupe for more than ten years.
- 57 *marriage is absolute... separation*: Divorce was not allowed in France until 1884. At the time only a '*separation de corps et biens*' ('separation of body and goods') was possible, granted for chiefly adultery or desertion.
- 61 *the only restaurant in the village*: The word '*gargotier*' is used, rather than 'restaurant', which suggests this is a very cheap-and-cheerful restaurant – a 'greasy spoon' or 'hash house'.
- 62 *The carriage... was an elegant one*: A *char-à-bancs*, which is a sort of covered wagon, with two parallel rows of seats.
- 65 *Émerainville*: An area to the east of Paris.
- 67 *stamped all over with baggage marks*: An allusion to the French railway porters' custom of gumming address labels to baggage at the time.
- 70 *A shadow passes... of despair*: The shadows are Doña Sol's despairing lovers, who fear she has been killed on her voyage.
- 77 *Everything passes... runs out*: A poetic idiom ('*tout passe, tout casse, tout lasse*').

77 *Souvenir of... Giffard*: Everyone who ascended in Monsieur Giffard's '*ballon-captif*' was given a medal. On one side is the balloon, and on the other is the inscription: '*Souvenir de mon ascension dans le grand ballon-captif à vapeur de M. Henry Giffard*'. Bernhardt made many ascents, so would have had many medals.

77 *The Invalid... Béranger*: A reference to the poem '*L'Invalide*' by the French poet Pierre-Jean de Béranger (1780–1857), in which one of the war veterans at Les Invalides in Paris bemoans his once plump form, his formerly well-shaped leg (shot away in the country's service) and his misspent time.

78 *How much I regret... misspent*: As with the earlier poem, some liberties are taken in the translation; '*mon bois si dodu*' has been given as 'not bent' rather than 'so plump' for the sake of the rhyme. Bernhardt also substituted '*bras*' ('arm') for '*bois*' ('wood') in Béranger's verse:

> Combien je regrette
> Mon *bois* si dodu,
> Ma jambe bien faite,
> Et le temps perdu!

# *A Biographical Note on Sarah Bernhardt*

Henriette-Rosine Bernard was born, it is thought, in October 1844. It can never be known for certain, as her birth certificate was lost in the fire at the city archive, when the Paris Commune torched the Hôtel de Ville in May 1871, and her various stories about her early life don't necessarily align.

The name of Bernhardt's father is not known, but she was born to Youle (Judith) Bernard, a young Dutch Jewish woman. While simplistic to label Youle a courtesan, she did keep the company of wealthy young men, who paid her way. She also ran a salon, which attracted men of great standing, including the composer Rossini, the novelist Dumas *père* and Charles de Morny (the half-brother of Napoleon III).

Bernhardt was sent off aged three to live with a nurse in Brittany; however, with her mother visiting her frequently, it was felt, according to the biography by Louis Verneuil, that she ought to be closer at hand, so it was only a few years until Bernhardt was moved to Neuilly, just outside Paris. Disaster struck, however, according to Bernhardt's own memoirs, when the nurse's husband died. She remarried and moved with Bernhardt into a cramped apartment in Paris; it soon transpired that all contact with Bernhardt's family had been lost, until one day her aunt Rosine happened to pull up in front of her building. Not believing that her aunt would return to collect her the next day as promised, Bernhardt threw herself in front of the carriage, breaking her arm in two places and injuring her knee. Youle soon returned to collect her, and Bernhardt spent the next two years recuperating.

Now aged seven, Bernhardt was sent off to the fashionable nearby boarding school, Madame Fressard's, just to the west of Paris. Here her education took off, and she soon learnt to read and write. She enjoyed her time at the school, and spoke highly of visits from a young actress from the Comédie-Française, who read poetry to the young girls. It appears that Bernhardt was visited by her mother – apparently once joined by de Morny – and by her father, who decided to move her to the Grandchamps Convent in Versailles, so that she could be brought up a Catholic. She stayed at the convent for six years under the watchful eye of Mother Ste. Sophie, who, Bernhardt reports, 'tamed' her.

Now aged about fifteen, Bernhardt's future was uncertain; her mother wanted her to marry into

Society, but Bernhardt was less convinced. After a fruitless conversation with a notary trying to give her advice, de Morny remarks that she should be taken to the Conservatoire, and so, not long later, young Bernhardt found herself at the Comédie-Française, in the box of Dumas *père*, where she was blown away by what she saw. In her memoirs, Bernhardt wrote of that evening, saying, 'This was the debut of my artistic life.'

Soon afterwards, Bernhardt auditioned for the Conservatoire, where (perhaps inevitably, supported as she was by the testimony of both de Morny and Dumas *père*) she was accepted straight away. It appears that she was a difficult charge, being forever late and tempestuous, but nonetheless she graduated in 1862, albeit with a somewhat mediocre report. To her delight, she was snapped up upon graduation by the Comédie-Française. Sadly, however, her sister Régine fell foul of one of the top actresses, who, in a brief altercation, Bernhardt slapped and swore at, and, refusing to apologise, was threatened by the management; she stormed out, tearing up her contract.

Almost immediately she found new employment, this time at the Gymnase theatre, where she stayed for a year; her mother spoke disparagingly about her performance, and the next day she sneaked out of the house with a maid and escaped for Spain. Some time later she returned to find her mother unwell; she had inherited some money from her grandmother, which allowed her to move with Régine to her own apartment. Not long after, in December 1864, her son Maurice was born. It is not certain who Maurice's father was – Bernhardt had had several lovers at this point, and liked to blur fact and fiction – but it is thought that the Belgian Prince de Ligne is the most likely candidate.

Finding herself out of work, without an income and with a young child, Bernhardt wrote to the Prince, whose reply was 'I know a woman named Bernhardt, but I do not know her child.' Nevertheless, he enclosed fifty francs – enough to warrant Bernhardt's trip to see him, where he rejected her. She is described at this point as living by her wits – surrounding herself with young men who paid her upkeep.

In 1866 Bernhardt wrote to a family friend who worked at the Théâtre de L'Odéon, and in August she resumed her career on stage. Her first night was not a success, and for the next year she was only given small parts, until almost a year later, when she 'was rewarded by three bursts of applause' for her part in Racine's *Athalie*. A little later, Victor Hugo's *Ruy Blas* was due to open, but was cancelled by the Government; instead, Bernhardt found herself playing a large part in a revival of Dumas' *Kean*. Outraged, a local group of students were up in arms, chanting that they wanted *Ruy Blas*, but Bernhardt strode on stage and accused them of hypocrisy for taking out their anger on Dumas. They soon settled down, and Bernhardt's name was burnished in the eyes of the management.

Not long after, while Bernhardt was dining with friends, her apartment went up in smoke; since she had no insurance at the time, she was forced to move back in with Youle, until a charity evening organised by a friend raised enough money that she was able to strike out alone once more. Her roles at the Odéon continued to grow in scope and acclaim, and by 1870 her prospects were looking very bright; but her career was brought to a sudden standstill with the arrival of the Franco-Prussian war.

Bernhardt rose to the occasion, and, with the closure of theatres in Paris due to the threat of invasion, she was instrumental in turning the Odéon into a hospital, where she worked as a nurse and fundraiser. The war was a difficult time that saw her cut off from her family and working hard in various hospitals in Paris, and these years left her changed for ever.

In 1872, following the squashing of the Paris Commune, the theatres were opened once more, and Bernhardt found herself in an important role in a staging of Hugo's *Ruy Blas* that had been banned years before. Her performance dazzled the crowd, and Hugo himself came backstage to thank her for her portrayal.

It was largely performances of this play that brought Bernhardt once more to the attention of the Comédie-Française, and overtures were made, leading to her departing the Odéon (in the middle of her contract, an act for which she was sued, and fined) for the Comédie-Française.

Here she went from strength to strength, wowing crowds in Racine's *Britannicus*, in Pierre Beaumarchais' *The Marriage of Figaro*, in Voltaire's *Zaïre* and in Racine's *Phèdre*. She became known for her *Phèdre* performance, which ran for many years.

In 1877, she had another success as Doña Sol in *Hernani* (see note to p. 12), a tragedy by Victor Hugo, who had by now become her lover. It was at about this time that she was taken in a balloon over Paris with Georges Clairin, another of her lovers, inspiring her to cast Doña Sol in *In the Clouds*. It soon became clear that she was not made for secondary roles, and she needed the limelight.

With the theatre in dire need of repairs, the director, Perrin, made a deal with London's Gaiety Theatre to transfer the company for a season; Bernhardt immediately spotted the potentially lucrative sideline she could carve out, performing in drawing rooms in wealthy Londoners' homes. Perrin tried to limit this sideline, which infuriated Bernhardt; she immediately resigned, but the Gaiety threatened to cancel the arrangement without her, so Perrin was forced to beg Bernhardt to withdraw her resignation – which came at the cost of making her a *sociétaire* (see second note to p. 53).

Bernhardt and their company were met in England by a whirlwind of publicity and a host of the theatre world's greatest names, including Oscar Wilde, who met her off the boat. After a shaky first night, Bernhardt took the London stage by storm, and she was a regular guest in the parlours of the wealthiest families in town – a fate which was sadly not shared by the rest of the company.

In the mean time, the French press had taken against Bernhardt, and were running a flak campaign; in a fury, she wrote a letter to *Le Figaro* in which she formally resigned from the company, and she deserted Paris with a maid for Le Havre. Assembling a troupe of her own, she returned to London, where she was a tremendous success. Ignoring overtures from the Comédie-Française who implored her to return, she toured Brussels, Copenhagen and France, before setting sail for New York in 1880. Her reception in America was slightly less enthusiastic at first, with critics decrying the acting of Bernhardt's supporting actors (a view she shared).

Nonetheless, the tour was a great success, and lasted a full seven months, in which time Bernhardt gave countless performances, interviews and endorsements. She returned to France exhausted but wealthy, and a household name around the world.

Back in Paris, the press had again taken against her, and she took once more to the stage at the Comédie-Française to clear her name. She embarked upon a European tour, where royalty including the Spanish king and the tsar praised her and bestowed compliments and gifts on her. It was on this tour that Bernhardt fell in love with Jacques Damala, whom she married. Although Bernhardt tried to help Damala's career, his plays flopped, he insulted her publicly and he eloped with an actress to Monte Carlo, where he lost a large sum of money by gambling, which Bernhardt was forced to cover. Although she sent him away, he returned, and she put up with him until his death in 1889, despite the fact that she loathed the very sight of him.

In 1883 Youle died, leaving Bernhardt distraught. Meanwhile, she had taken over a theatre to provide roles for Damala and a managerial position for her son, Maurice; the theatre did terribly, and lost a substantial amount of money, forcing Bernhardt to auction off her jewels to avoid insolvency. Against this backdrop, interspersed by brief sojourns in Paris, she spent the next few years on tour across the Americas and Europe – and even Australia, where she delighted crowds, although there seems to have been an anti-Semitic preoccupation in the press with her Jewish heritage.

In 1893 she took over the lease of the Théâtre de la Renaissance, where she ran everything, directing, producing and starring in productions in between her tours for the next six years, when she gave it up in favour of a larger theatre (now the Théâtre de Ville), which was renamed Théâtre Sarah Bernhardt.

In 1899 came one of her most important roles, in a newly translated (and long, at four hours) production of *Hamlet*. This production, while successful in drawing large crowds in Paris and on tour, divided the critics, and caused uproar. Notwithstanding this, she continued the performances, and her *Hamlet* was even filmed in 1900.[1]

The last years of the nineteenth century saw her in a slew of new roles, including Goethe's Werther, Hugo's Lucrezia Borgia and Wilde's Salomé (although this didn't make it to the stage, as it was banned in England).

All this travelling and acting had taken its toll, and Bernhardt's health declined; a knee injury became so painful that, in 1915, she had it amputated. Determined to keep her positivity, she planned lecture tours, and threw herself into imagining new possibilities. Crutches and wooden legs were tried and rejected, and

---

[1] At the time of writing, a short clip of a fencing scene can be found on YouTube.

eventually she settled on using a sedan chair, on which she was carried.

Having been moved from Paris in the run-up to the First World War, Bernhardt returned in 1915, determined to help in some way. Although she was unable to take up the nursing duties she had assumed in her youth, she decided she could perform for the troops – against the advice of the Government, and despite her now advanced age and poor health. Witnesses wrote that Bernhardt performed out in the open to three thousand soldiers at any given time, and ended her performances with singing the *Marseillaise*, raising huge cheers.

At this time, Bernhardt was making films, and it was against the war-torn scenes that some of them were made, touring villages decimated by bombing.

In 1916, Bernhardt set off for America for a final tour, hoping to convince the country to join the war. While no longer able to act out full plays, she chose acts that she was able to perform, and toured the country to great acclaim, until a sudden illness in 1917 brought things to a halt, and she had to undergo surgery. Recovering swiftly enough, and afforded great inches of newspaper columns, Bernhardt returned to France in 1918, wealthy and beloved, to news of the end of the war.

At this time, Bernhardt was teaching at the Conservatoire as well as touring and managing her theatre, and continued to perform in films. Achieving recognition for many of her roles, it was really *Elizabeth, Queen of England* in 1912 that put her on the map, earning her the title of 'the first international movie star'. As well as performing well financially, the film was considered important for making film more attractive to committed theatre-goers who had previously been sceptical.

Her health continued to deteriorate, and her reputation came to suffer, with critics considering her finest work as belonging to a past era. Nonetheless, she continued undaunted, refusing her son's insistence that she should retire.

On the 26th of March 1923 Bernhardt died. France was distraught: news reached her theatre in the middle of a performance, and the curtain was lowered and the audience left quietly. Her funeral was arranged by the Parisian local government, and was attended by hundreds of thousands of people, who lined the streets.

Her legacy as the first international film star, one of France's most famous women, and one of the most fascinating personalities of all time endures to this day, and the name Sarah Bernhardt will likely always be associated with the great texts and productions she performed and inspired throughout her career.

## OTHER CLASSIC FICTION FROM RENARD PRESS

ISBN: 9781913724092
224pp • Paperback • £7.99

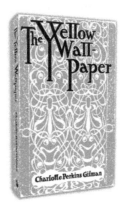

ISBN: 9781913724160
64pp • Paperback • £6.99

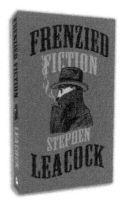

ISBN: 9781913724085
224pp • Paperback • £6.99

ISBN: 9781913724078
160pp • Paperback • £7.99

ISBN: 9781913724108
64pp • Paperback • £6.99

ISBN: 9781913724115
128pp • Paperback • £7.99

DISCOVER THE FULL COLLECTION AT
WWW.RENARDPRESS.COM